SCARY CANARY

by Robin Carly

pictures by Mort Gerberg

A LITTLE ROOSTER BOOK

A Trumpet Club Original Book
Bantam Doubleday Dell Publishing Group, Inc.
New York · Toronto · London · Sydney · Auckland

Scary Canary

A Little Rooster Book/September 1993

Co-published by Bantam Doubleday Dell Books for Young Readers,
a division of Bantam Doubleday Dell Publishing Group, Inc.,
and The Trumpet Club
1540 Broadway, New York, New York 10036

ISBN 0-553-37328-5

Created and produced by Chardiet Unlimited, Inc.
Based on the song "Scary Canary" by Mike Lobel.

Published simultaneously in the United States and Canada
PRINTED IN THE UNITED STATES OF AMERICA

1 3 5 7 9 10 8 6 4 2
UPR

"Mary, your birthday is coming," Mom said.

"What do you want for a present?"

"A horse!" I said.

"Don't be silly," Dad said.

"We don't have room for a horse.

Get a little pet."

"I'll take a dog. Marcie has a dog."

"Marcie's mother is home all day," my mom said.

"Sarah has a cat. I'll have a cat."

"No," Dad said. "I'm allergic to cats.
How about a goldfish?"

We went to the pet store.

The goldfish were pretty.

But then I heard a bird singing

"Tweet-tweet, tweet-tweet."

"That's a canary," the pet-store man said.
"Canaries are very friendly and tame.
They'll even perch on your finger."

"That's the pet for me," I said.

As soon as we got home, I called my best friend, Sarah. She came right over to see my bird.

"What's his name?" Sarah asked.

"I don't know yet," I said.

I opened the cage. The bird flew out and perched on my finger.

"He's cute," Sarah said. "Why don't you call him Cutie, or Sweetie? Or Tweety, or Tiny, or . . ."

"No," I said. "Those are ordinary names. He needs a special name. One that's just right for him."

The canary flew back into his cage.

"He needs toys to play with," Sarah said.

We ran upstairs to find toys for the cage.

"Come down in five minutes, girls," Mom called out.
"It's almost dinner time. I'm making spaghetti."

Mom was in the kitchen.

The spaghetti was almost done.

She took some parsley for the sauce

from the mini plant grower.

Just then the phone rang.

The canary flew into Dad's newest invention—
the Perfecto Plant Grower.
Mom didn't see him, so she closed the door.

The warning light went on.

Suddenly there was a loud noise
and a flash of light.
Sarah and I came running.

"Oh, no!" Mom yelled.

My canary was in the plant grower!

Mom opened the door, and my canary flew out.

Finally he lit on my hand. His feathers
were sticking out in all directions. But
he wasn't hurt at all. He just looked scared.

I put him in his cage. I put my toy mouse in, too.

"Here's a friend that's just your size."

"It will keep you company," I said.

Then I locked the cage
so he wouldn't get into trouble.

The next morning my canary looked bigger.

"It's just your imagination," said my mom.

"Come eat your breakfast."

But the day after that, there was no doubt.
The bird *was* bigger.

By the end of the week,
he barely fit into his cage.

"This is *not* a normal bird," Dad said.

We went to the vet. "He's a canary, all right. But I've never seen one that big."

"Maybe we should take him back to the pet store," my mom said.

"Good grief!" the pet-store man said.

"Canaries never get that big.

Let me give you another one instead."

"No," I said. "We just need a bigger cage."

My canary got bigger every day.

The more he grew, the more he ate.

His chirping got louder, too.

It was more like barking.

Dad was not happy. "He makes too much noise
and he costs too much money to feed."

Mom wasn't happy either. There were
feathers all over the house.

Finally there was no cage big enough to hold the canary. We had to put him in the garage and park the car on the street.

"I'm sorry, Mary," Dad said. "Your canary is bigger than a horse. We said you could have a *little* pet. We just can't keep him anymore."

That night a thief came down the street.

He wanted to steal our car.

But my canary saw him
and flew out of the garage.
The robber went screaming for help.

The canary was chirping as loudly
as he could. All that noise woke us up.
Dad called the police. They came right away
and captured the crook.

The policeman said, "I've never heard of
a watchbird before. You're a lucky family."

Even the thief agreed. "That's some scary canary."

"Does that mean we can keep him?"

Dad said, "Yes."

I hugged my bird.
"You've got a home.
You've got a job.
And now you've got a name . . .
SCARY CANARY!"